Over the River
and Through the Wood

Over the Rive

nd Through the Wood

Lydia Maria Child
illustrated by Iris Van Rynbach

MULBERRY BOOKS, New York

First Mulberry Edition, 1992. Printed in the U.S.A.

10 9 8 7 6 5 4 3 2 1

ISBN 0-688-11839-9

Library of Congress Cataloging-in-Publication Data
Child, Lydia Maria Francis, 1802-1880.
[Boy's Thanksgiving Day]
Thanksgiving Day/by Lydia Maria Child; illustrated by Iris
Van Rynbach.
p.   cm.

Text originally published in v. 2 of the author's *Flowers
for Children,* 1844, under title: A Boy's Thanksgiving Day.
Summary: An illustrated version of the well-known text
describing the joys of a Thanksgiving visit to
grandfather's house.
[1. Thanksgiving Day—Poetry.   2. Songs.] I. Van Rynbach,
Iris. ill. II. Title.
PZ8.3.C4335TH 1989
811'.2—dc19
LC 88-4712
CIP
AC

For Vicki Martin Guertin

and

Karen Klockner

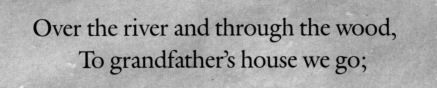

Over the river and through the wood,
To grandfather's house we go;

The horse knows the way
To carry the sleigh
Through the white and drifted snow.

Over the river and through the wood —
Oh, how the wind does blow!

It stings the toes
And bites the nose,
As over the ground we go.

Over the river and through the wood,
To have a first-rate play.
Hear the bells ring,
"Ting-a-ling-ding!"
Hurrah for Thanksgiving Day!

Over the river and through the wood
    Trot fast, my dapple-gray!
    Spring over the ground,
    Like a hunting-hound!
For this is Thanksgiving Day.

Over the river and through the wood,
    And straight through the barn-yard gate.

We seem to go
Extremely slow, —
It is so hard to wait!

Over the river and through the wood —
Now grandmother's cap I spy!

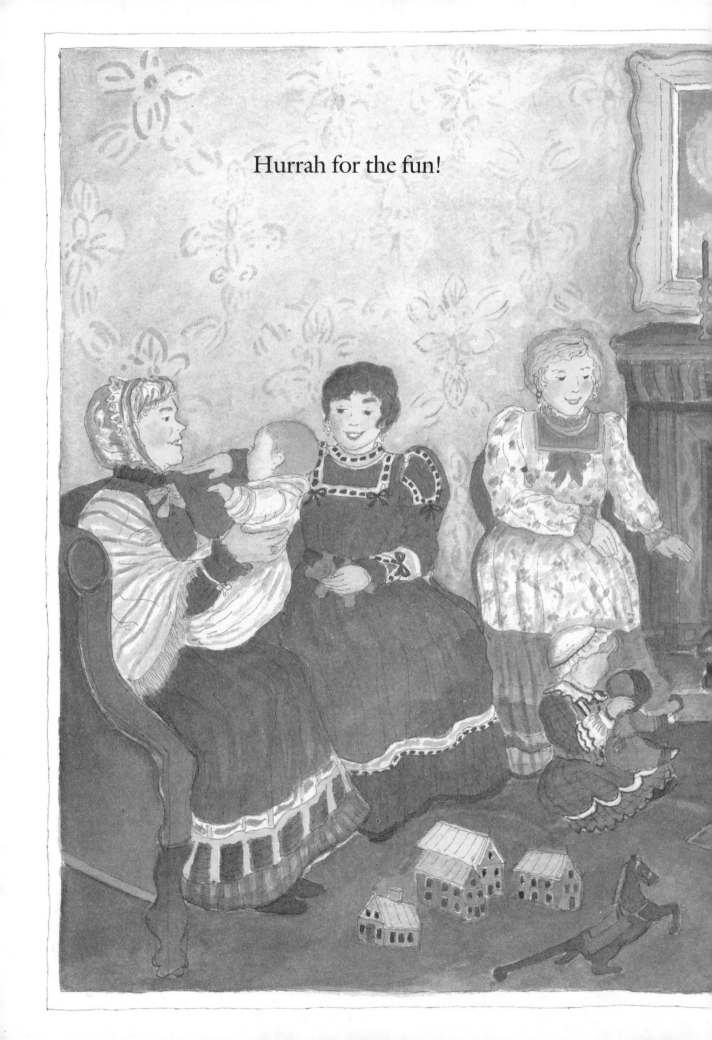

Hurrah for the fun!

Is the pudding done?

Hurrah for the pumpkin-pie!